KU-165-733

READ with me!

First words
a pre reader

by WILLIAM MURRAY
compiled by JILL CORBY
illustrated by CHRIS RUSSELL

Ladybird Books

Kate

40p

READ with me! *has been written using about 800 words and these include the 300 Key Words.*

In the first six books, all words introduced occur again in the following book to provide vital repetition in the early stages. The number of new words increases as the child gains confidence and progresses through the stories. After Book 6, a wider range of vocabulary is used but each word is repeated at least three times within that story.

The stories centre on the everyday lives of Kate, Tom, Sam the dog, Mum, Dad, friends, neighbours and relations. This setting often provides a springboard into Tom and Kate's world of make-believe. Also, the humorous, colourful illustrations include picture story sequences to stimulate the reader's own language and imagination.

A complete list of stories is given on the back cover and suggestions for using each book are made on the back pages.

Further details about this reading scheme plus a card listing the 300 Key Words are contained in the Parent/ Teacher Guide.

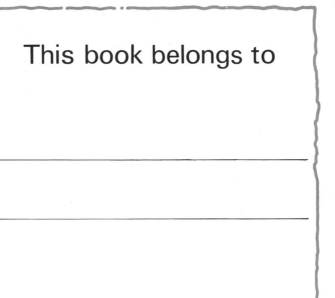

This book belongs to

_____

_____

British Library Cataloguing in Publication Data
Murray, W. (William), *(date)*
    First words.
    1. English language—Readers
    I. Title   II. Corby, Jill   III. Russell, Chris   IV. Series
    428.6
    ISBN 0-7214-1338-2

First edition

Published by Ladybird Books Ltd Loughborough Leicestershire UK
Ladybird Books Inc Auburn Maine 04210 USA

Printed in England (7)

Tell the story.

What will happen next?

Tom

Tell the story.

What will happen next?

Sam

Tell the story.

Where is Sam's bone?

Dad

Mum

John

Suki

Lucy

Here is Tom.

Under a stone where the earth
                     was firm,
Tom found a wiggly, wriggly worm.
"Good morning," he said.
"How are you today?"
But the wiggly worm just
                     wriggled away.

Here is Kate.

Which is different?

Which two are the same?

Tell this story.

Find these pictures in the story.

Talk about the picture.

How many things of each colour can you count?

Tell the story.

Do you know this story?

Talk about this picture.
Which animals are watching
Little Red Riding Hood?

What belongs to Kate, John, Suki and Tom?

Which one is different in each row?

Talk about this picture.
Where is Sam?

How many mice can you find?

Kate and Tom
like the ball.

Find six differences in this picture.

Notes for using this pre reader

Learning to read requires many more skills than just decoding the words on the page. Also a child needs to be ready and keen to learn to read in order to progress with enjoyment and confidence. The points listed below will help you to check your child's readiness for reading:

1 *Can your child see and hear properly?*
2 *Does your child ask questions, does he* want to know about the objects and things happening around him?*
3 *Does your child understand spoken instructions and can he carry them out?*
4 *Does your child listen to a story?*
5 *Can your child retell a simple story in a fairly logical sequence?*
6 *Can your child see similarities and differences in simple drawings?*
7 *Does your child draw recognisable objects?*
8 *Is your child fairly self-reliant and able to work alone for short periods?*
9 *Can your child match identical shapes?*
10 *Does he show signs of wanting to read, asking what words mean, and pretending to read from books?*

If the answer to the majority of these questions is yes, then your child will probably be ready to start on a reading scheme such as **READ with me!**

* *To avoid the clumsy he/she, him/her, we have referred to the child as ''he''. All the books are of course equally suited to both boys and girls.*